HEALING THE BRUISES

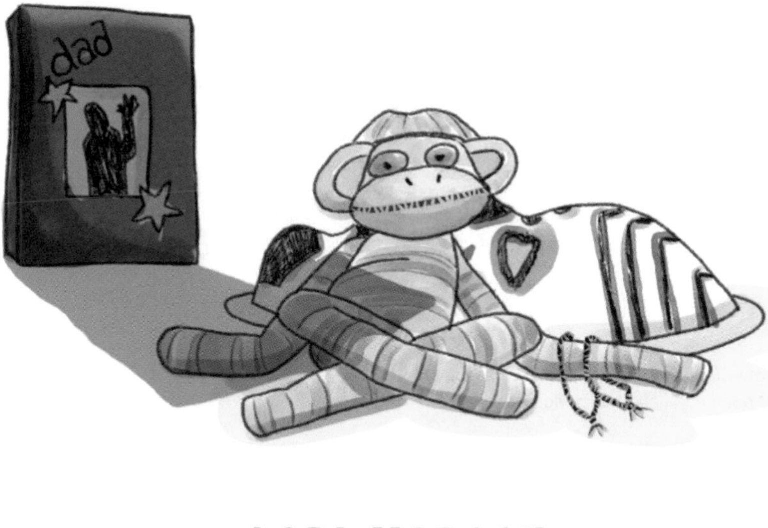
dad

LORI MORGAN

ILLUSTRATIONS BY KATHY KAULBACH

FORMAC PUBLISHING COMPANY LIMITED

Dedicated to the silenced children of domestic violence, who have yet to find their voice and discover their joy.

Text copyright © 2013 by Lori Morgan
Illustrations copyright © 2013 by Kathy Kaulbach

Formac Publishing Company Limited recognizes the support of the Province of Nova Scotia. We are pleased to work in partnership with the province to develop and promote our cultural resources for all Nova Scotians. We acknowledge the financial support of the Government of Canada through the Canada Book Fund for our publishing activities. We acknowledge the support of the Canada Council for the Arts, which last year invested $157 Million to bring the arts to Canadians throughout the country.

NOVA SCOTIA   The Canada Council | Le Conseil des Arts for the Arts | du Canada   Canada

Design: Kathy Kaulbach, Touchstone Design House
Editor and creative assistant: Jan Morrison

Library and Archives Canada Cataloguing in Publication data available

ISBN-13: 978-1-4595-0283-3

ISBN-10: 1-4595-0283-3

Formac Publishing Company Limited
5502 Atlantic Street
Halifax, NS,
Canada B3H 1G4
www.formac.ca

Printed and bound in Canada.

My name is Julia.
This is my story.

All my life my parents fought. I thought fighting was normal.

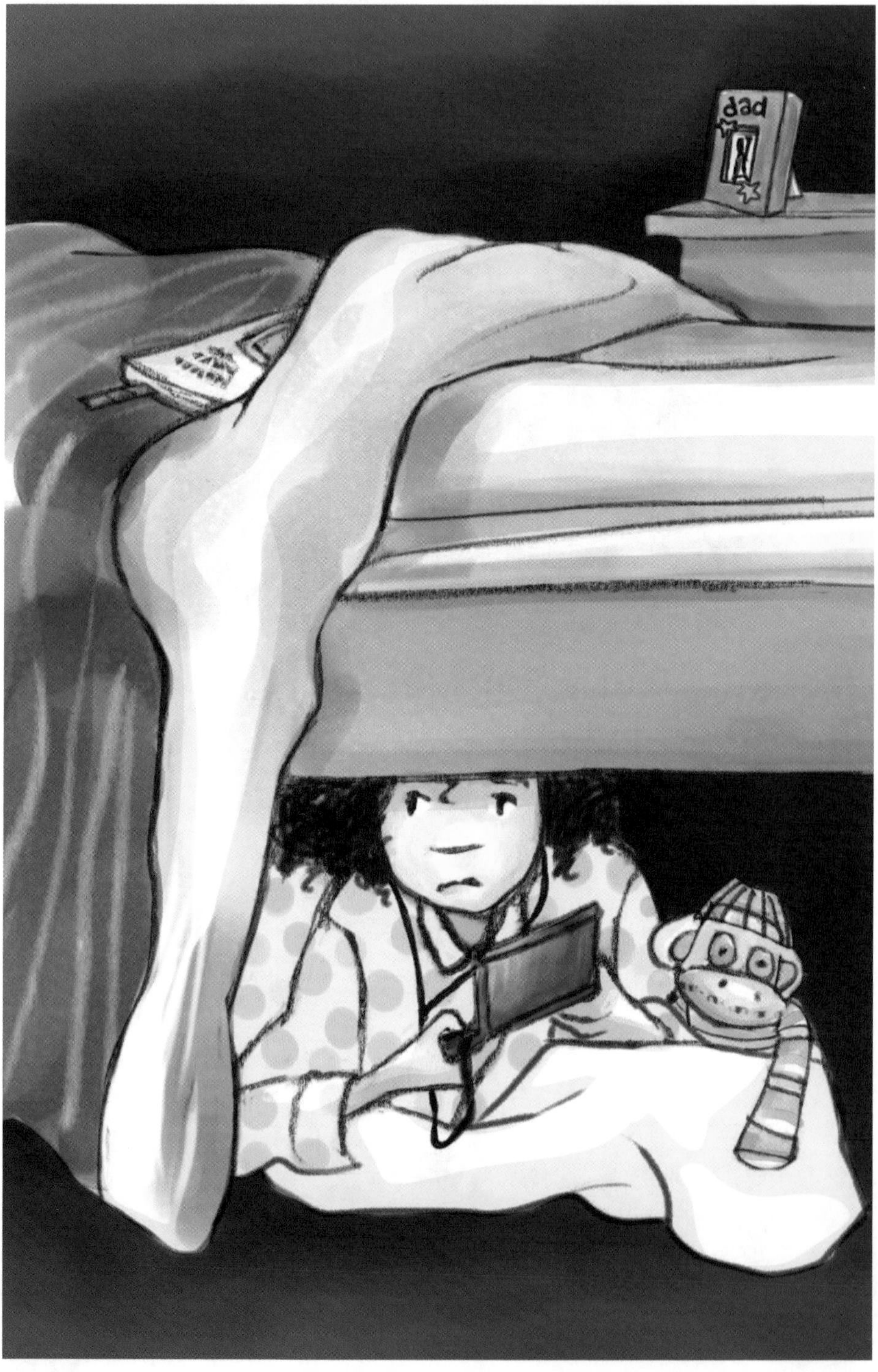
dad

Sometimes my dad pushed or hit my mom. She would hide the bruises with make-up or long-sleeves.

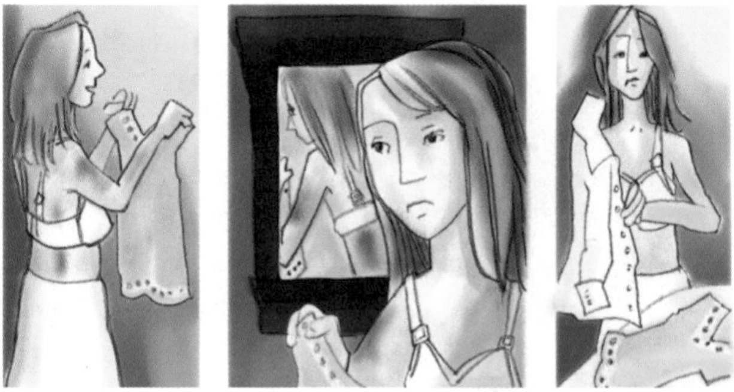

After a fight, Dad would leave our house. Those nights mom slept with me. We were both scared.

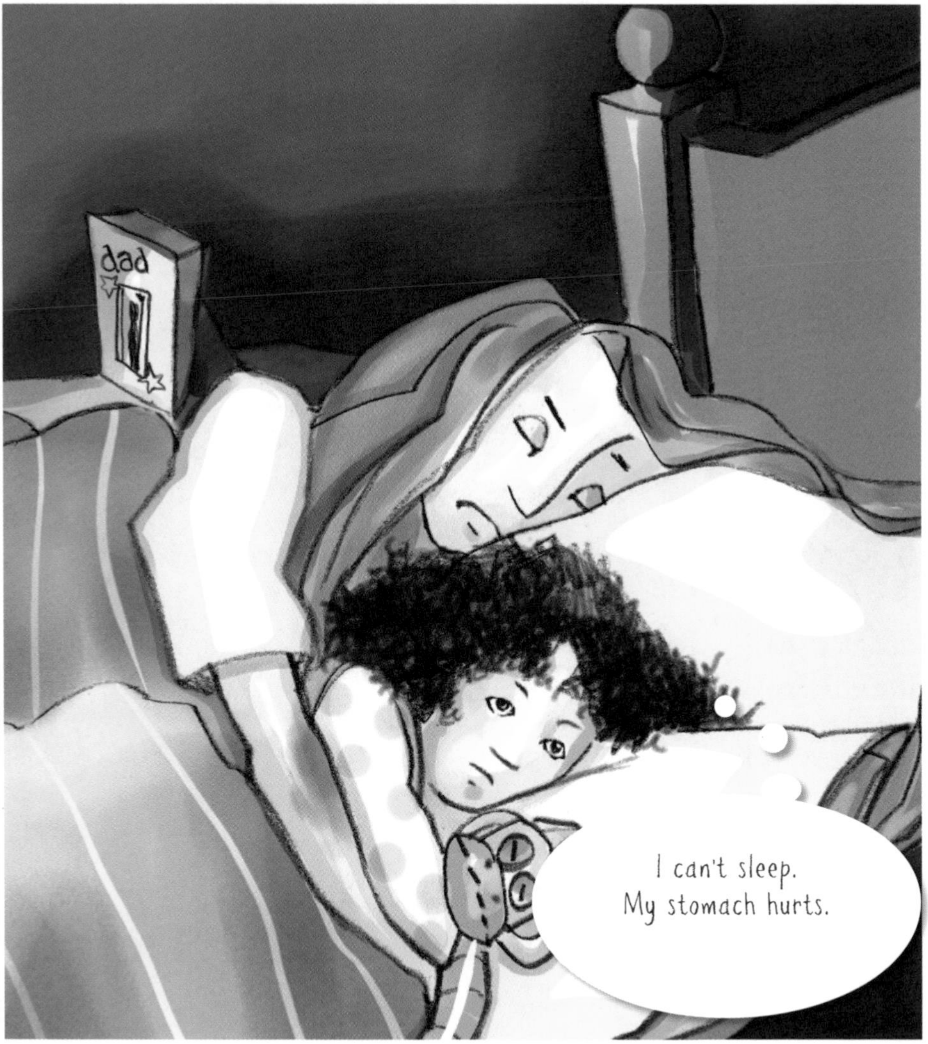
dad
I can't sleep. My stomach hurts.

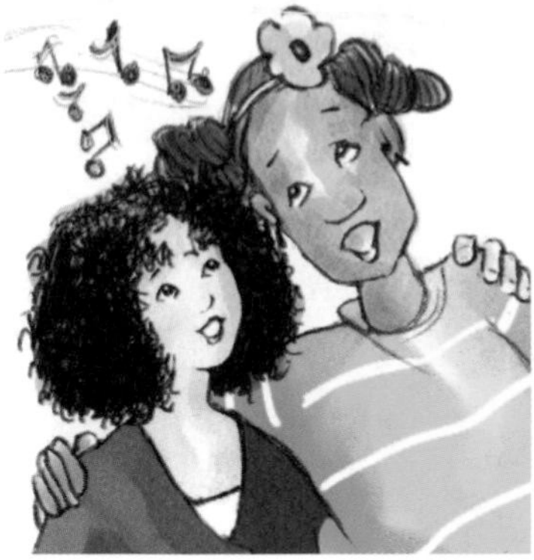

Every day, I walked home from school with my best friend Keisha. She was the only person I told about my mom being hurt. I knew I should tell someone else, but I felt ashamed.

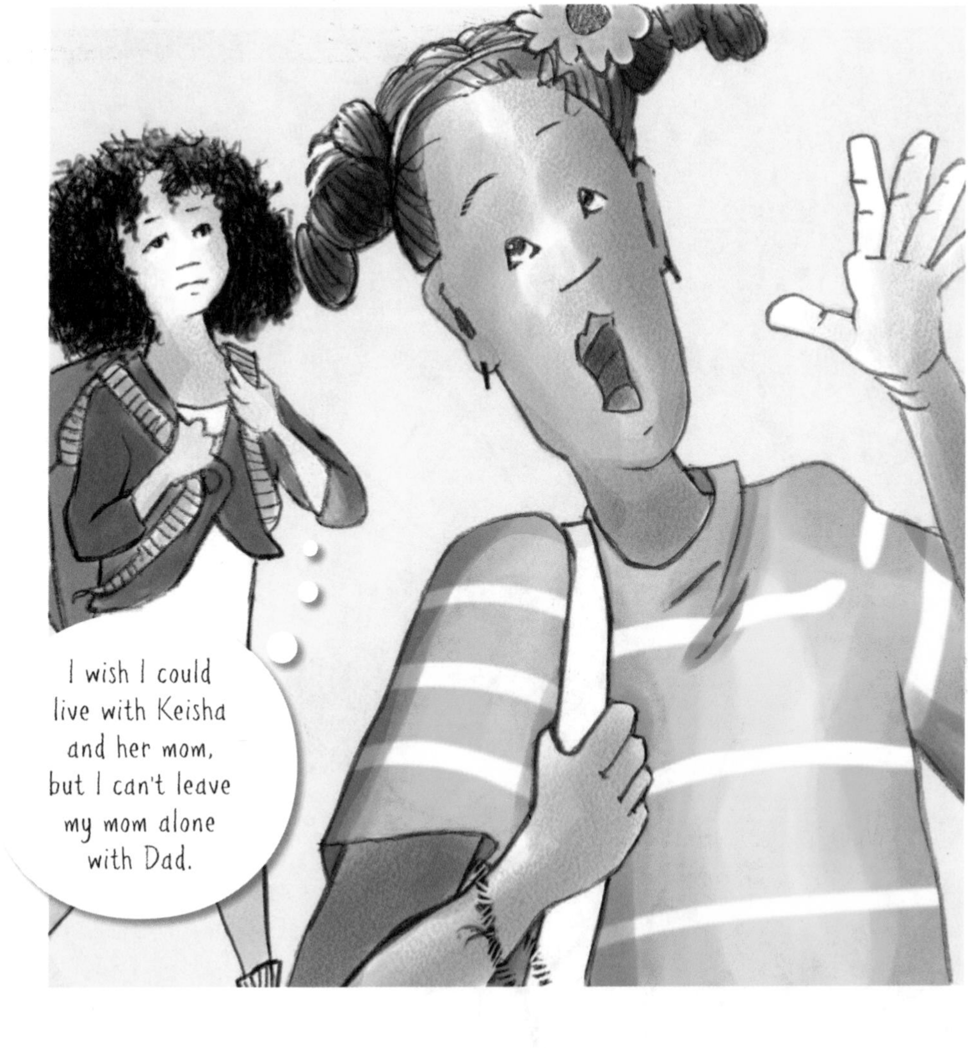
I wish I could live with Keisha and her mom, but I can't leave my mom alone with Dad.

When I was at school I felt tired. I couldn't concentrate. I got headaches. I wasn't hungry. And sometimes I got into trouble.

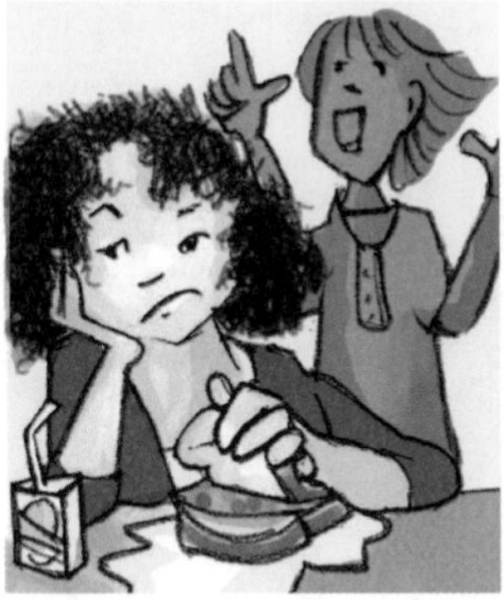

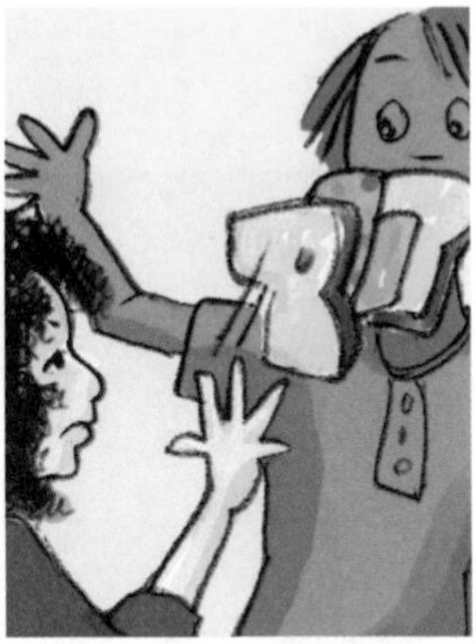

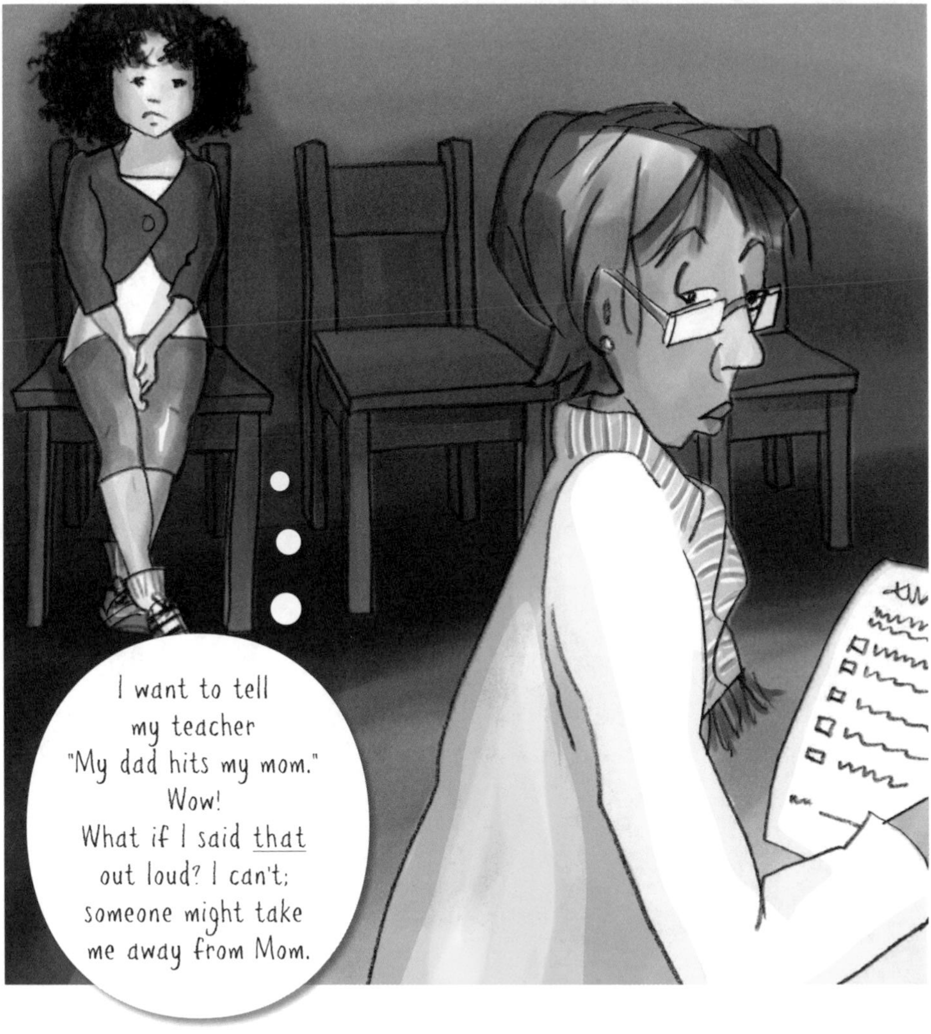
I want to tell my teacher "My dad hits my mom." Wow! What if I said that out loud? I can't; someone might take me away from Mom.

I got home from school one day and Mom had been crying.
She told me that this time we were leaving.

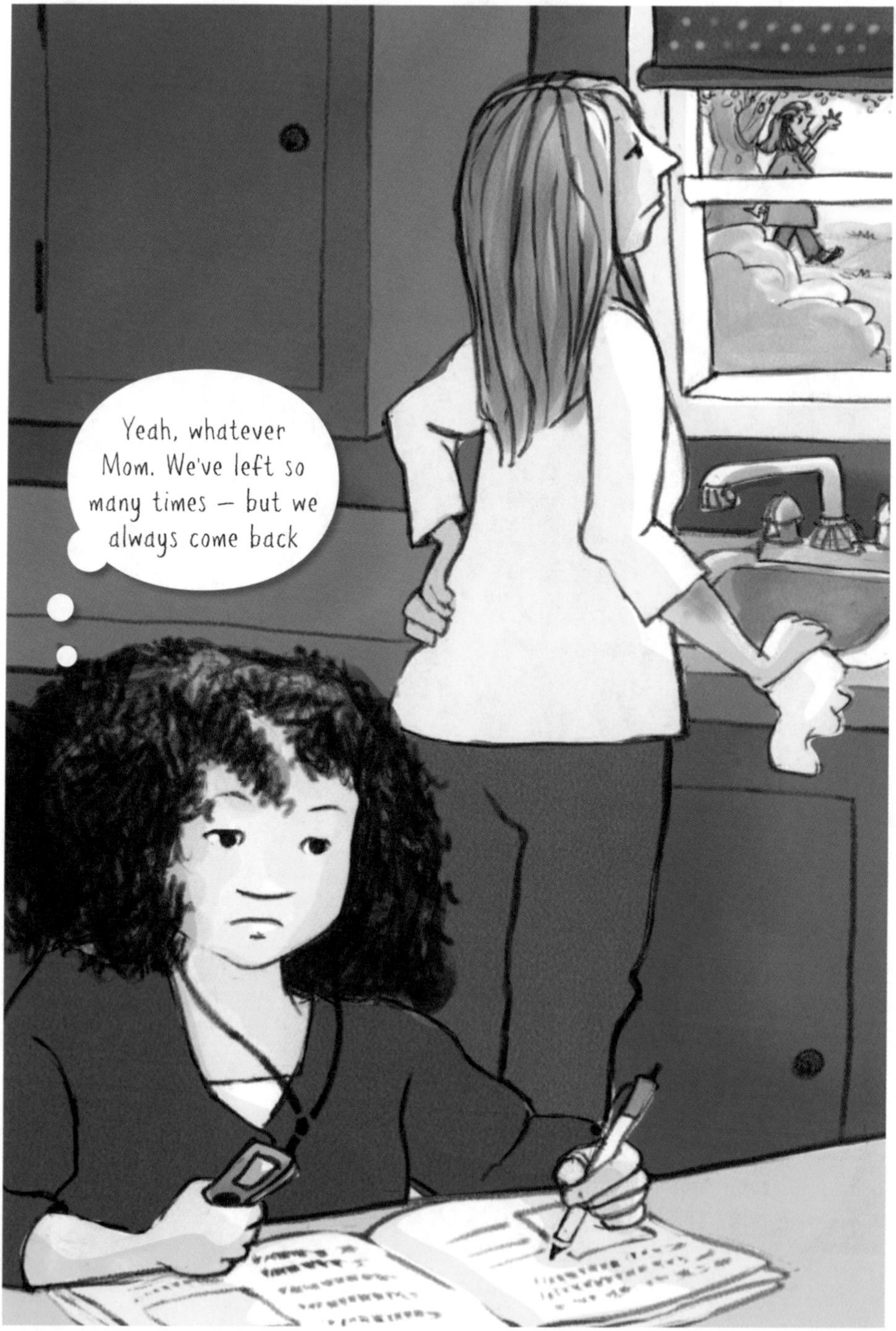
Yeah, whatever Mom. We've left so many times — but we always come back

Mom gave me a suitcase and told me to pack my favourite things.

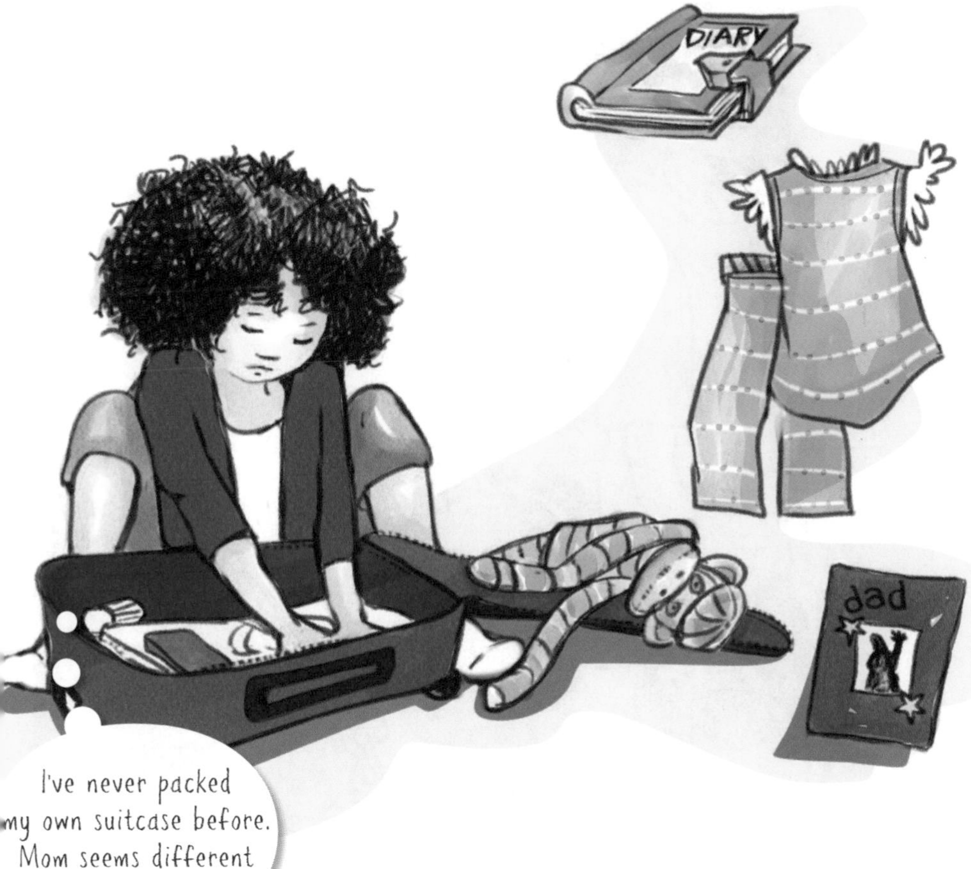
DIARY
dad
I've never packed my own suitcase before. Mom seems different this time.

Mom said we would be leaving later in the week. I could not tell anyone. It was a secret.

More secrets. I couldn't say goodbye to my friends or teachers. I couldn't even tell Keisha.

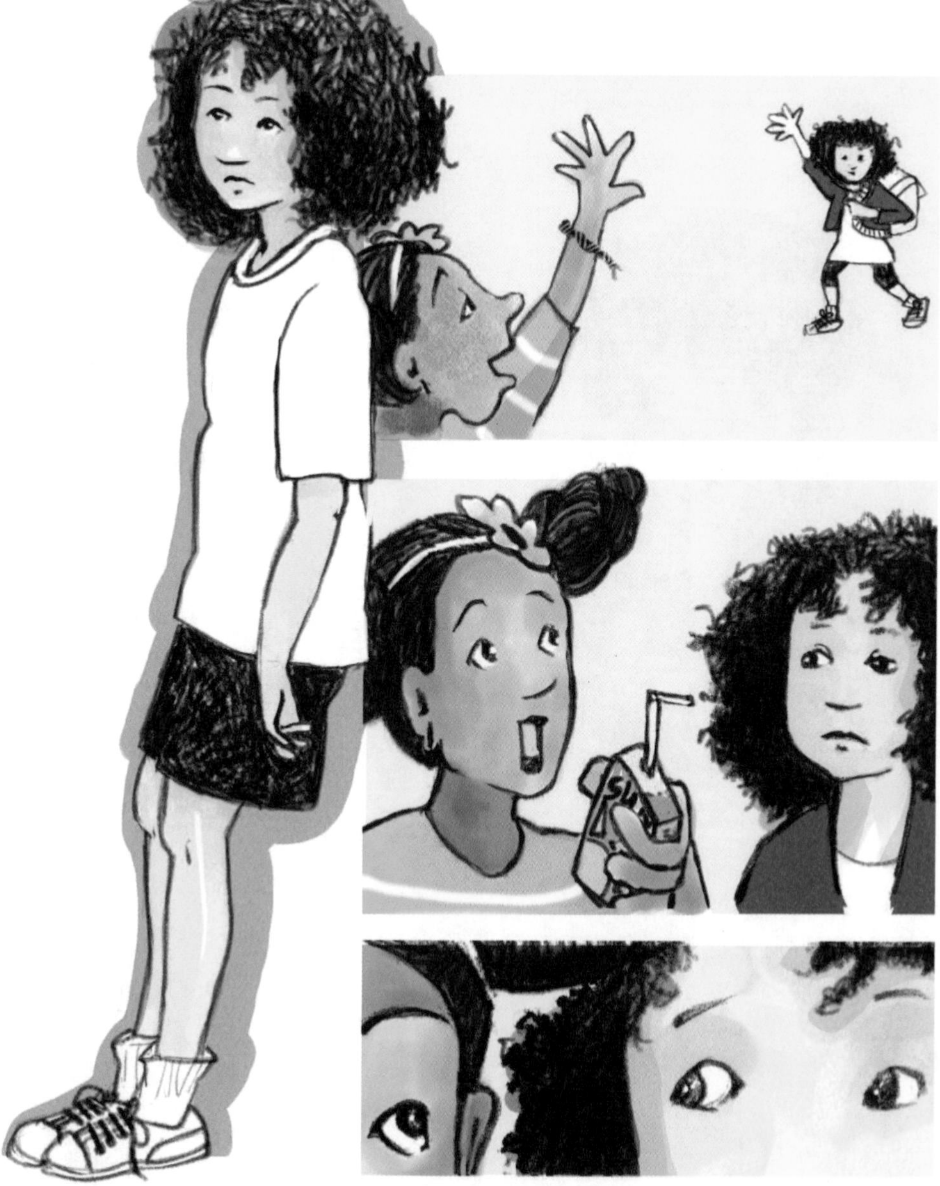

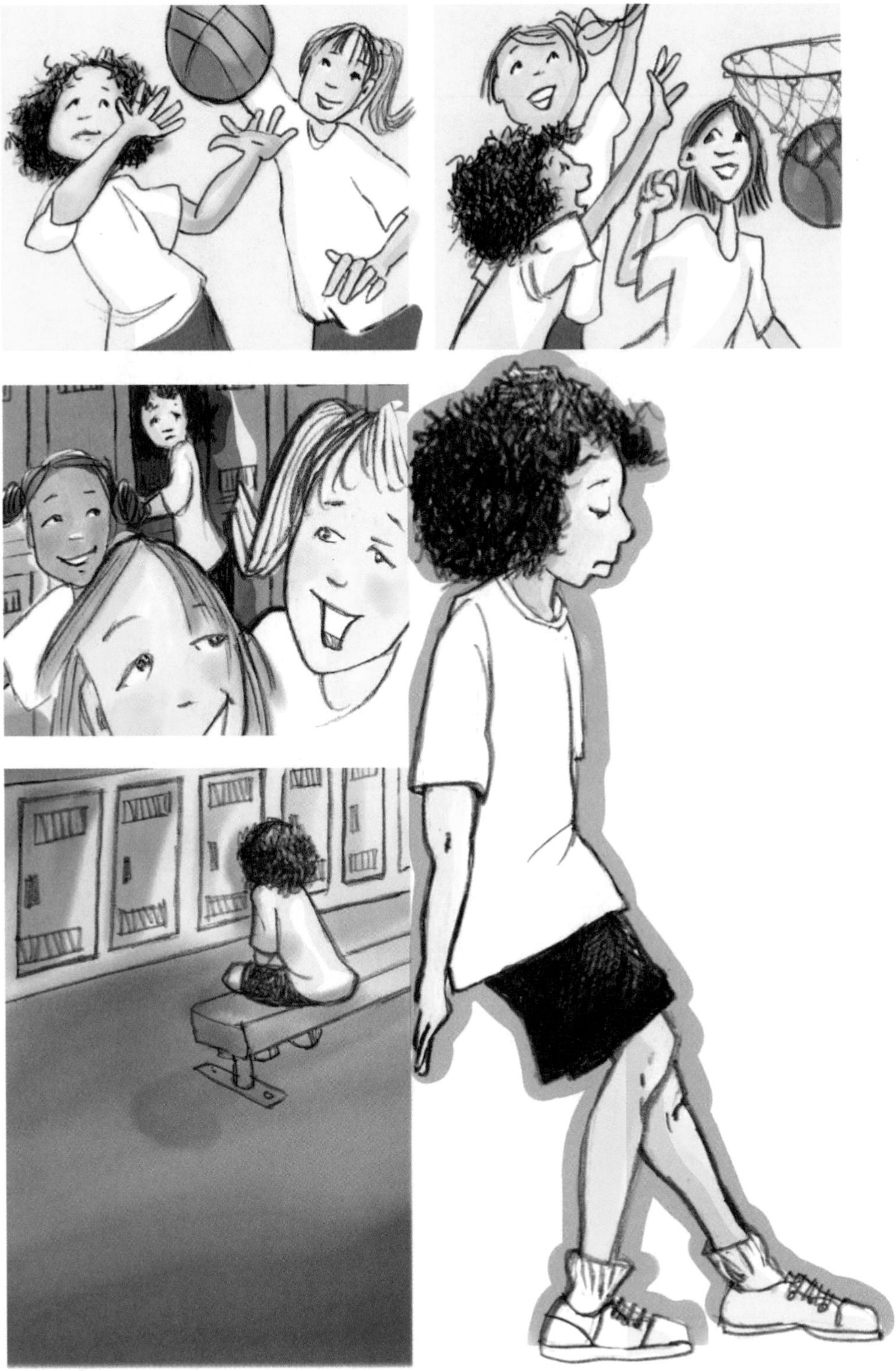

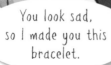

You look sad, so I made you this bracelet.

It was a long week.

The days passed and Mom didn't change her mind. This time it was for real . . .

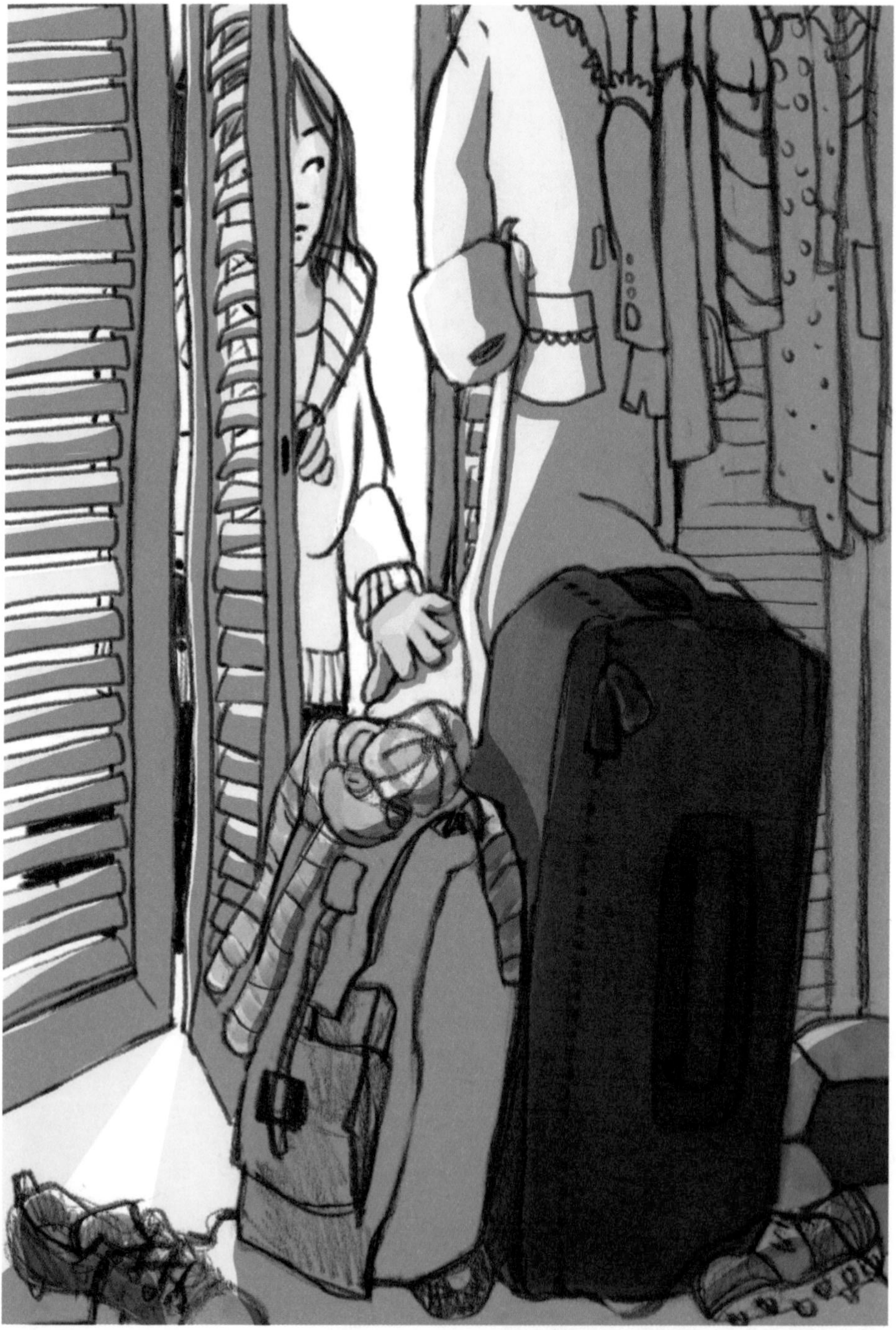

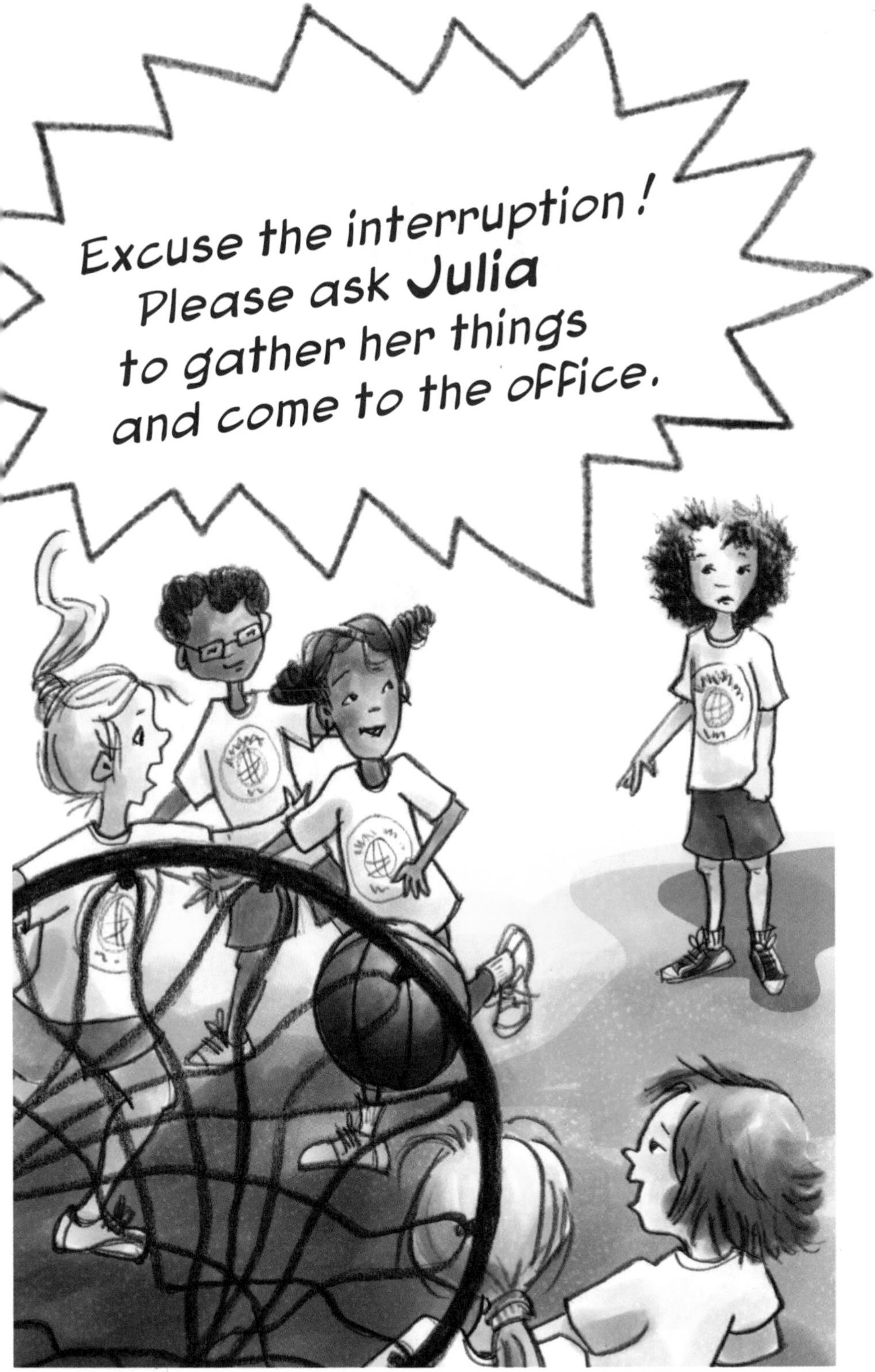
Excuse the interruption! Please ask **Julia** to gather her things and come to the office.

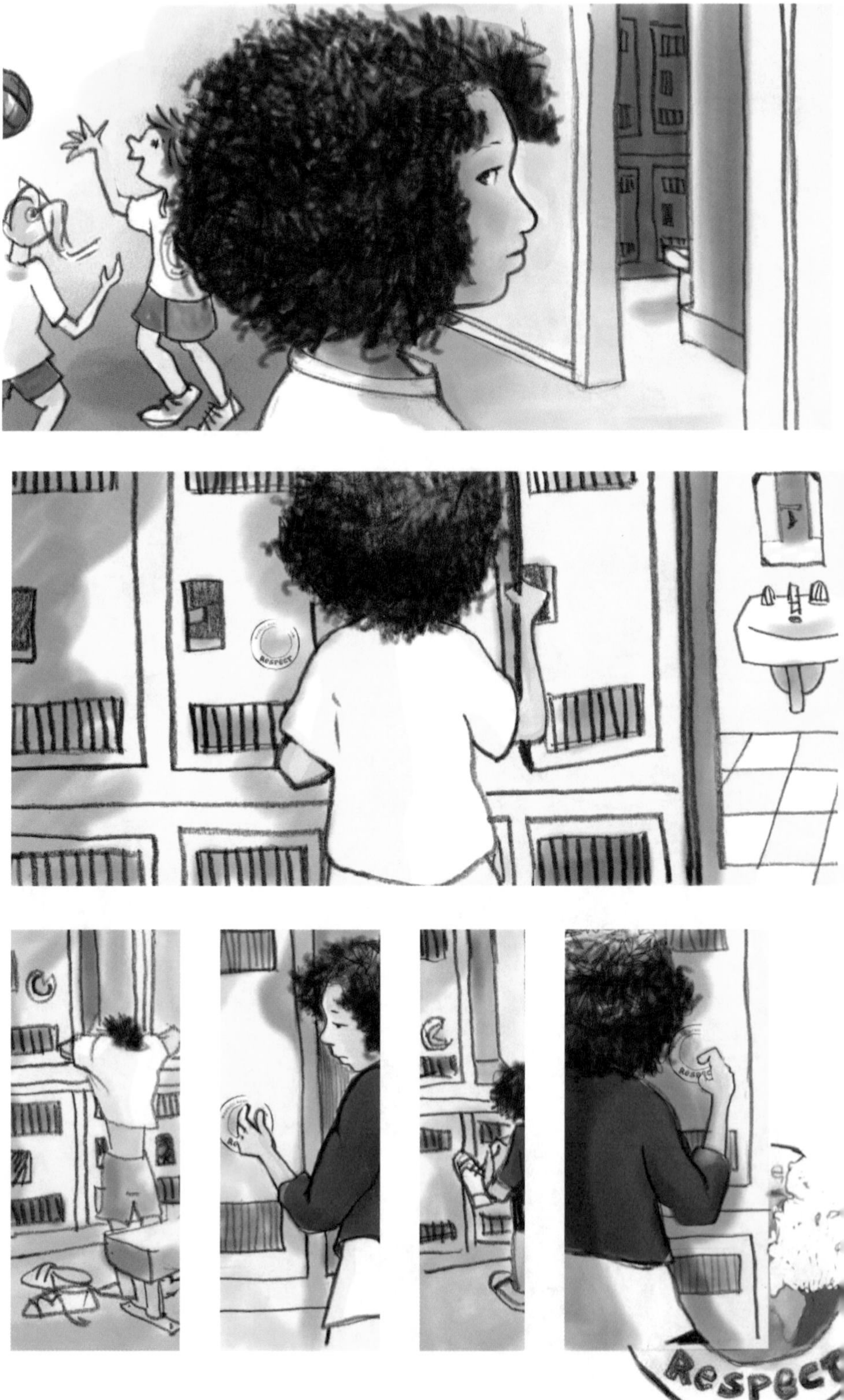

RESPECT
Respect

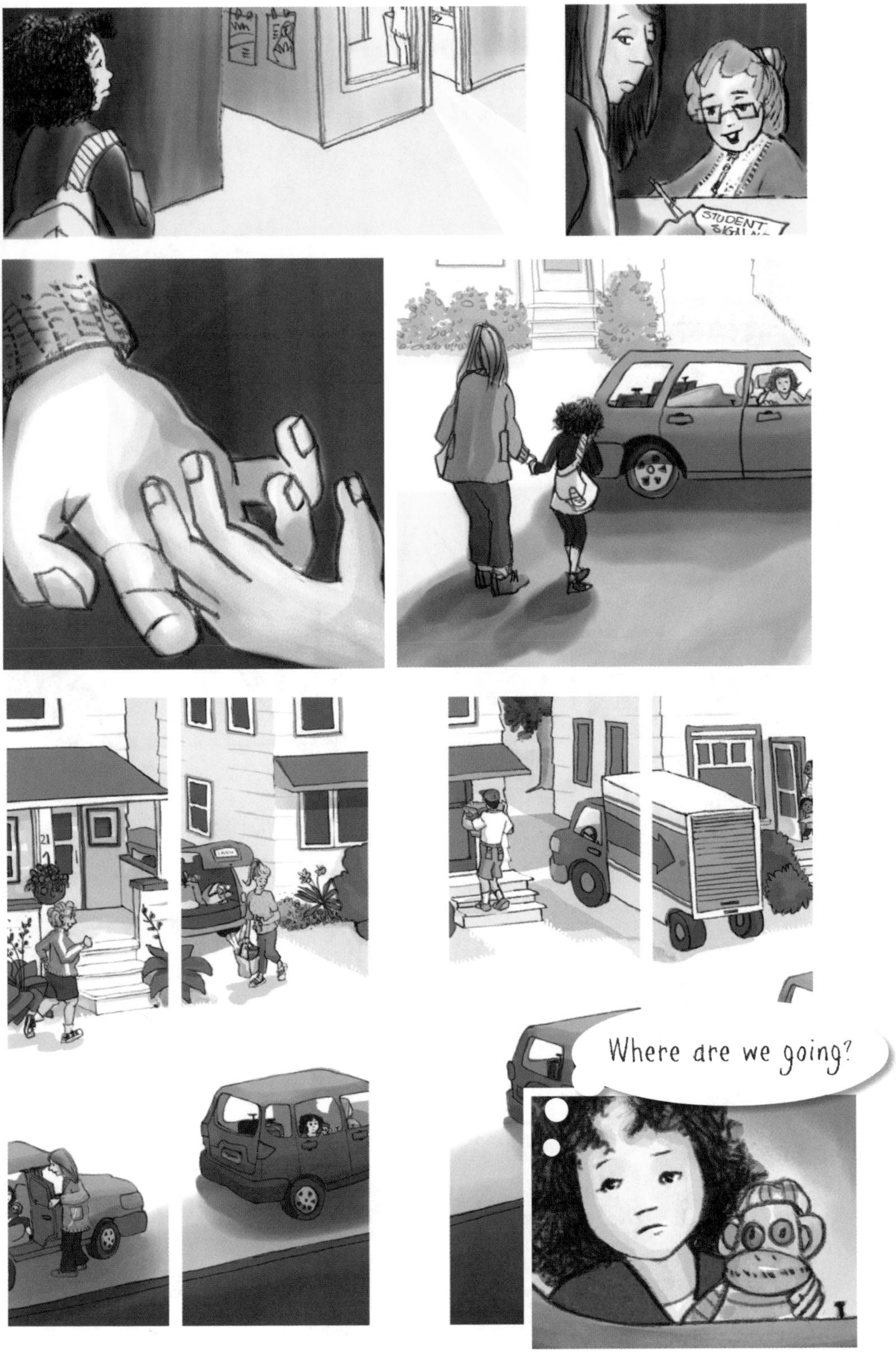
STUDENT
Where are we going?

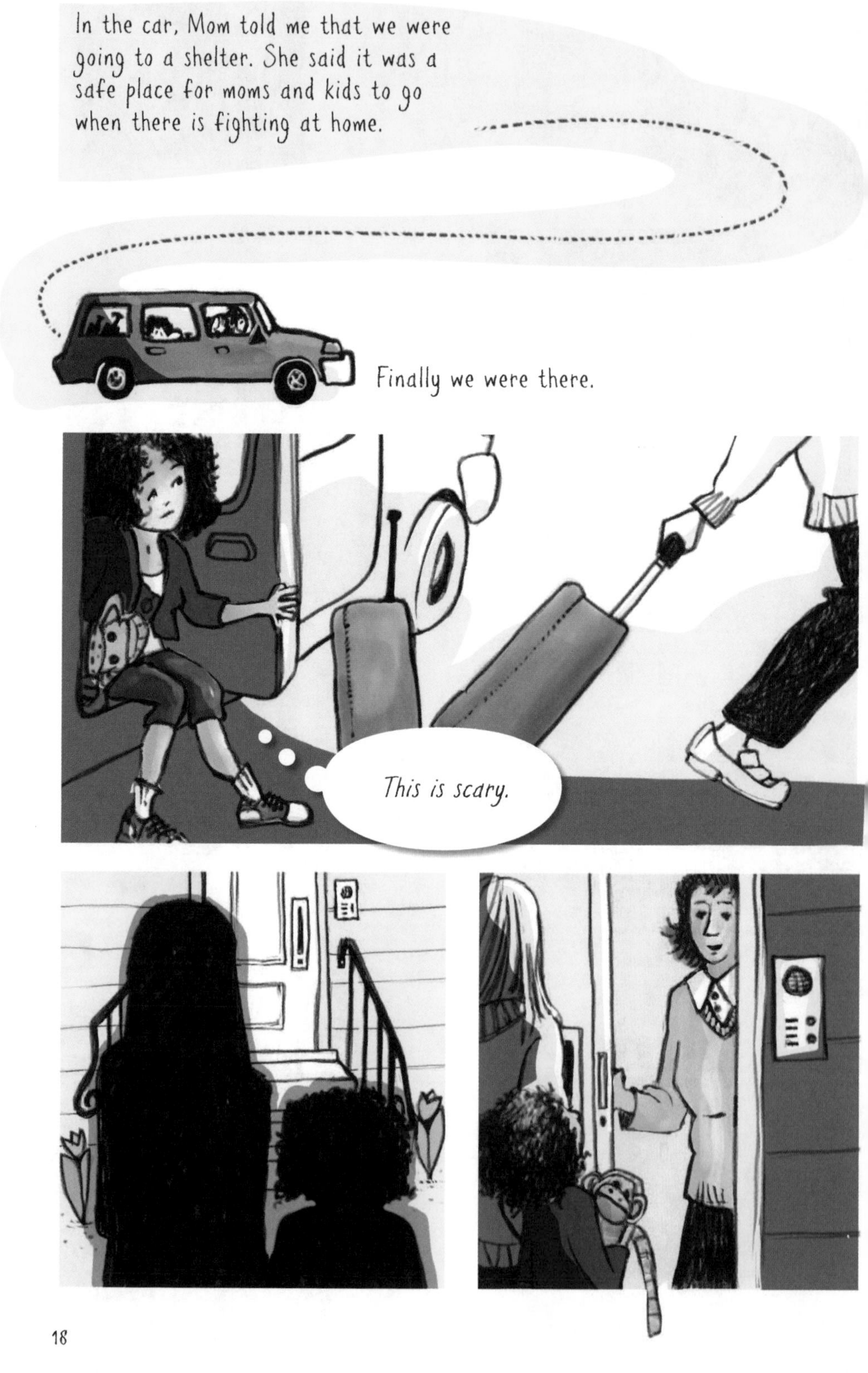
In the car, Mom told me that we were going to a shelter. She said it was a safe place for moms and kids to go when there is fighting at home.
Finally we were there.
This is scary.

"You must be Julia, I'm Mirella," said the lady who met us at the door. "Let's go to the kitchen for a snack while your mom takes care of a few things."

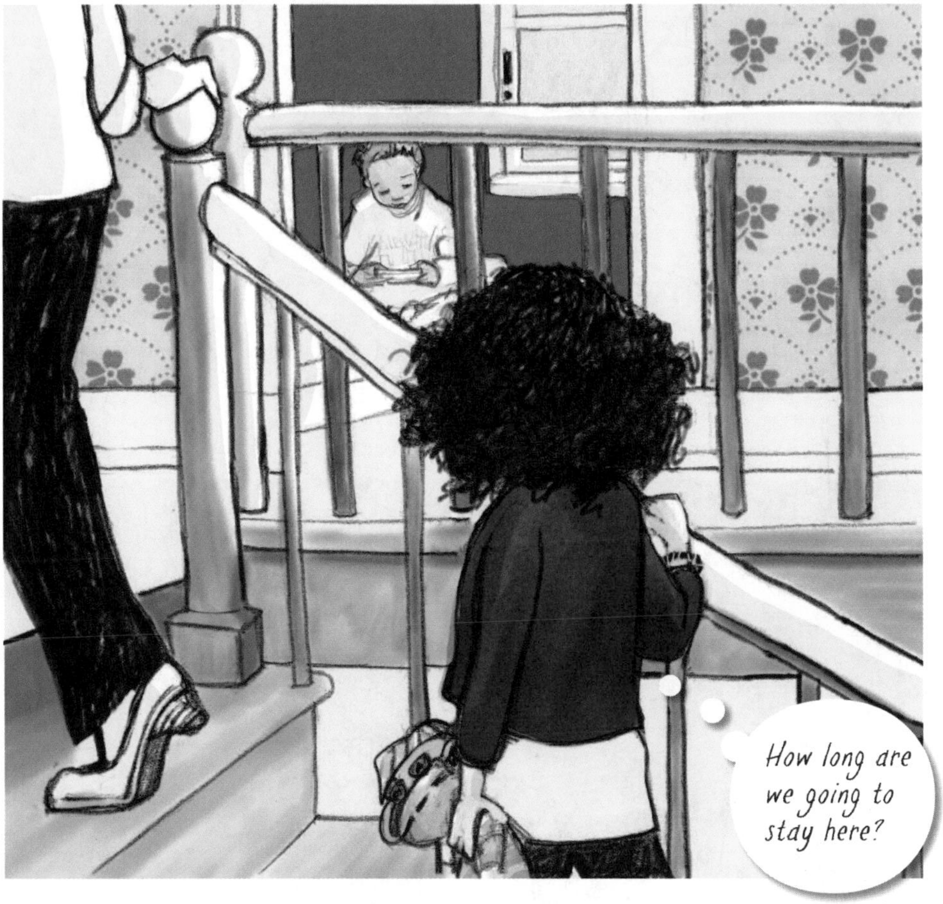
How long are we going to stay here?

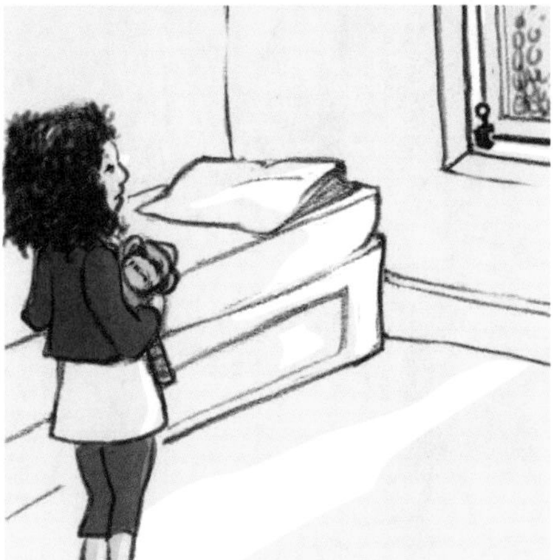

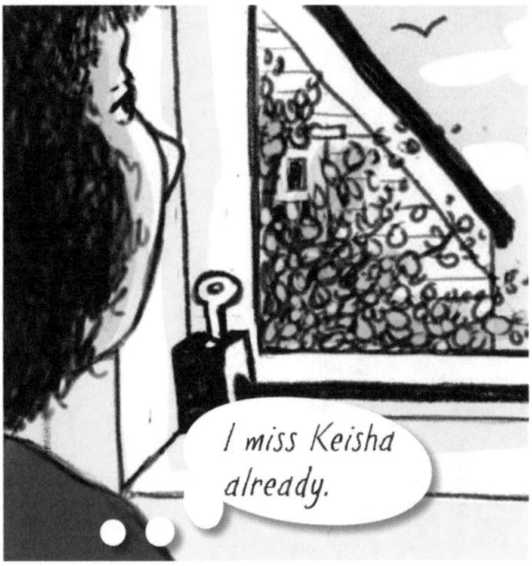
I miss Keisha already.

I felt safe at the shelter, but I missed Dad.

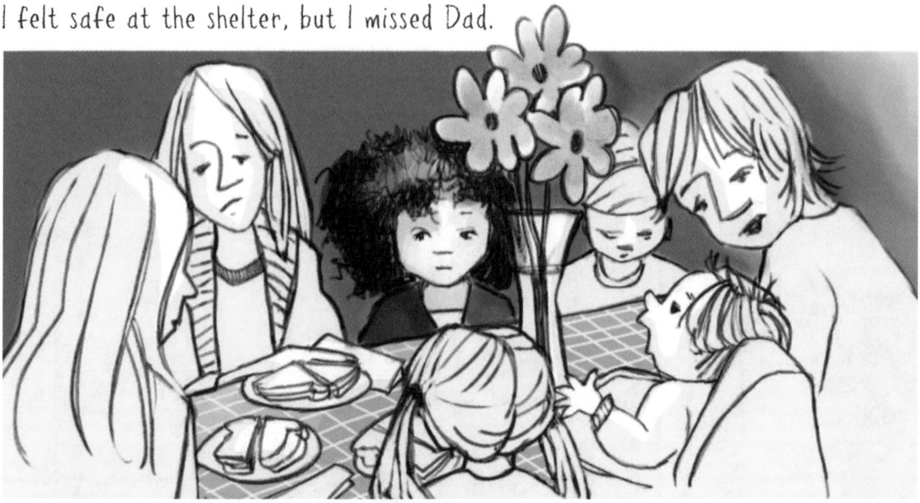

I couldn't believe how many other kids were there.

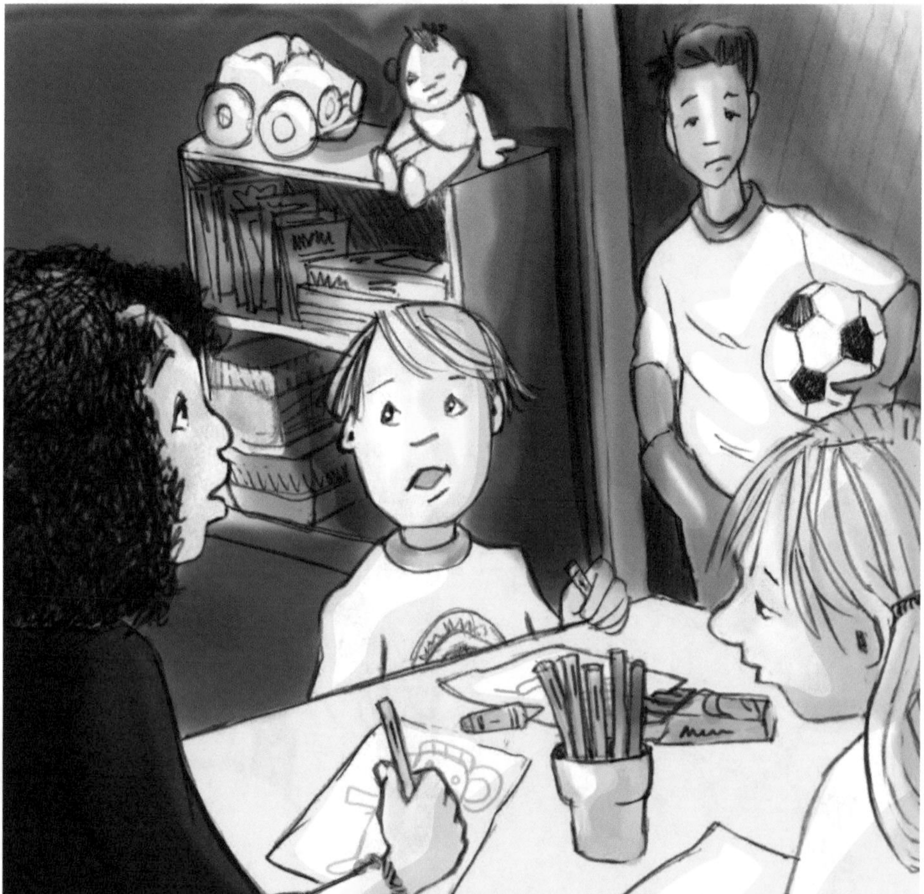

My favourite person was Emanuel. He was fun to hang out with and easy to talk to.

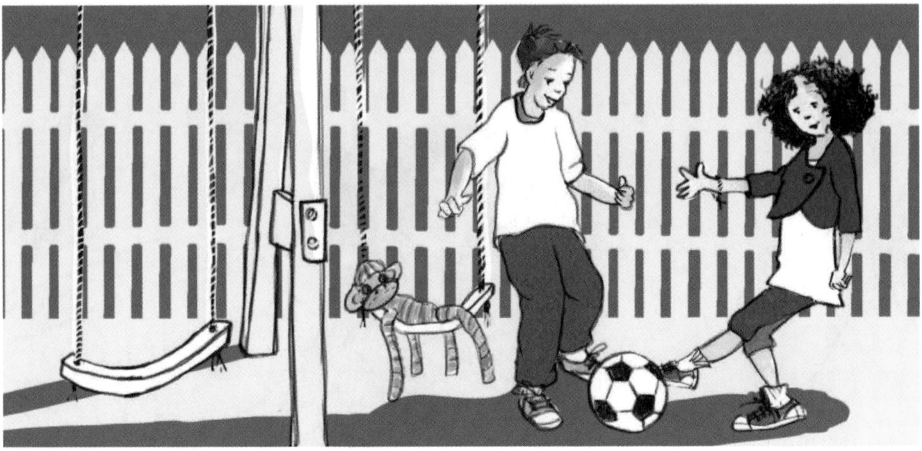

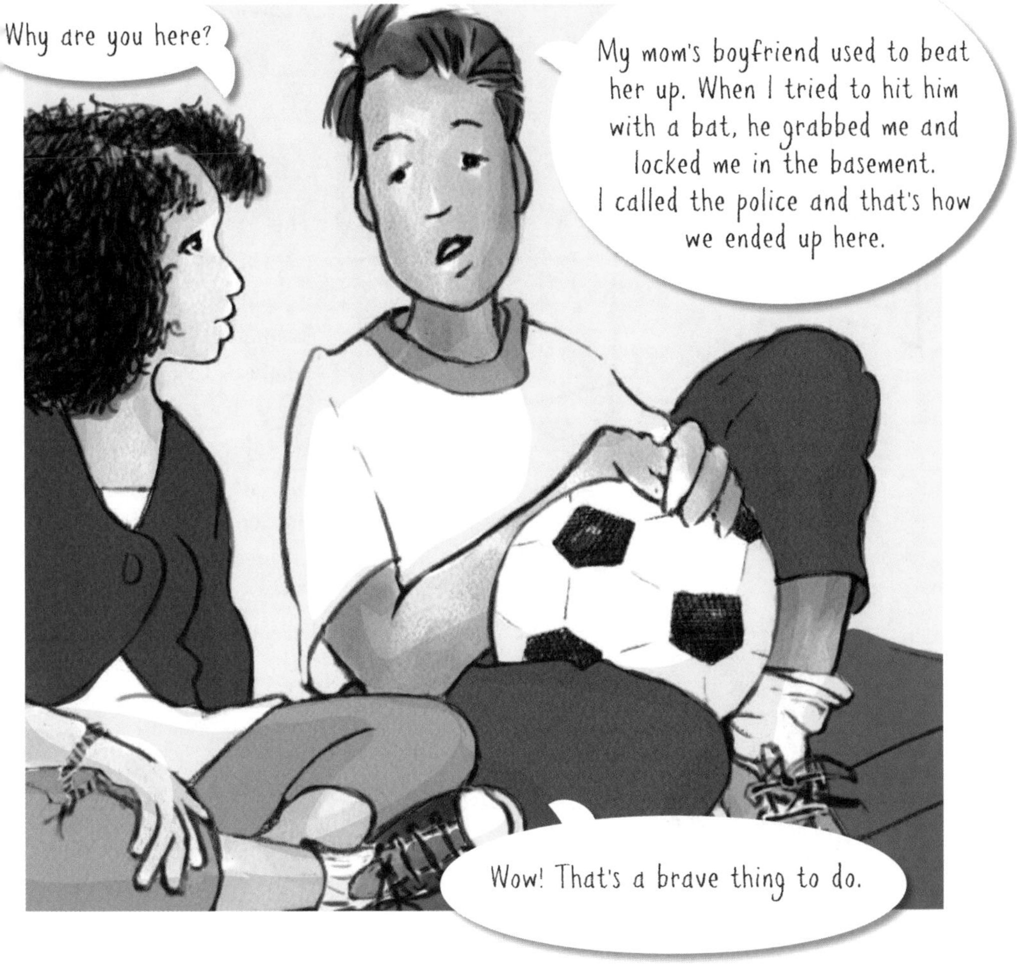
Why are you here?
My mom's boyfriend used to beat her up. When I tried to hit him with a bat, he grabbed me and locked me in the basement. I called the police and that's how we ended up here.
Wow! That's a brave thing to do.

We stayed at the shelter for three weeks. Sometimes Mom still cried, but her bruises were almost gone. One day she said we would be moving to something called safe housing.

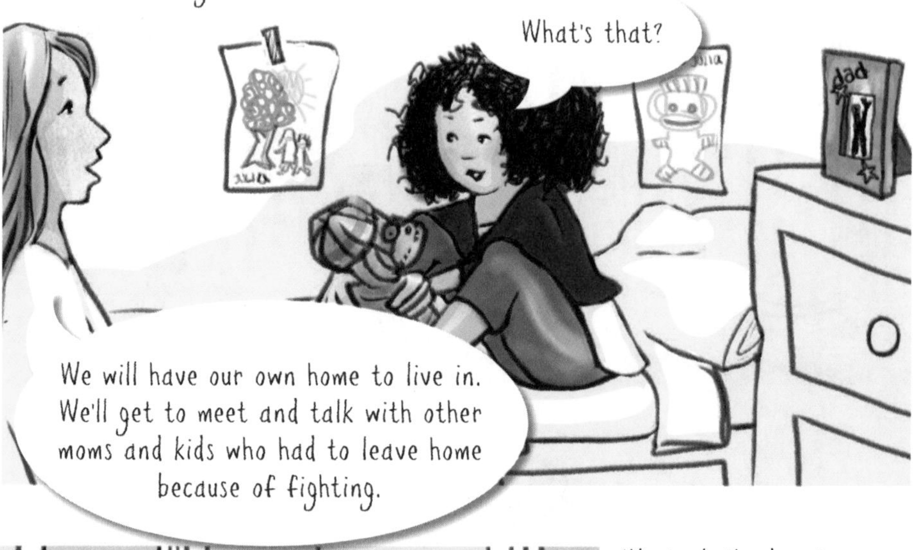

What's that?
We will have our own home to live in. We'll get to meet and talk with other moms and kids who had to leave home because of fighting.

We took the bus to see our new home.

The house seemed really empty, but I liked it. The woman who showed us around gave Mom phone numbers to help us get furniture and explained the alarm system. Mom said we had to stay at the shelter until our new stuff arrived at the house.

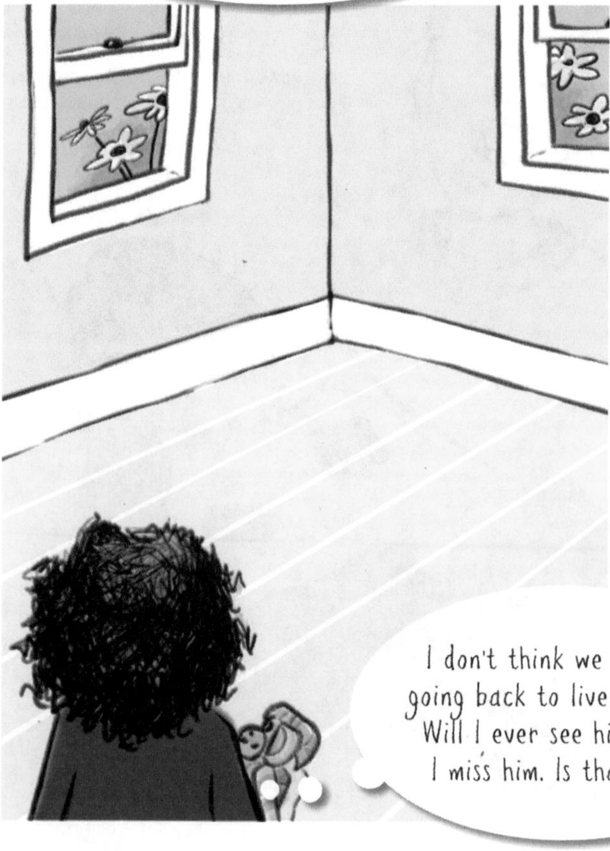

I don't think we are ever going back to live with Dad. Will I ever see him again? I miss him. Is that okay?

Emanuel and I spent all of our time together until I had to leave. Emanuel said that he and his mom would be moving in with his nana in a couple of days.

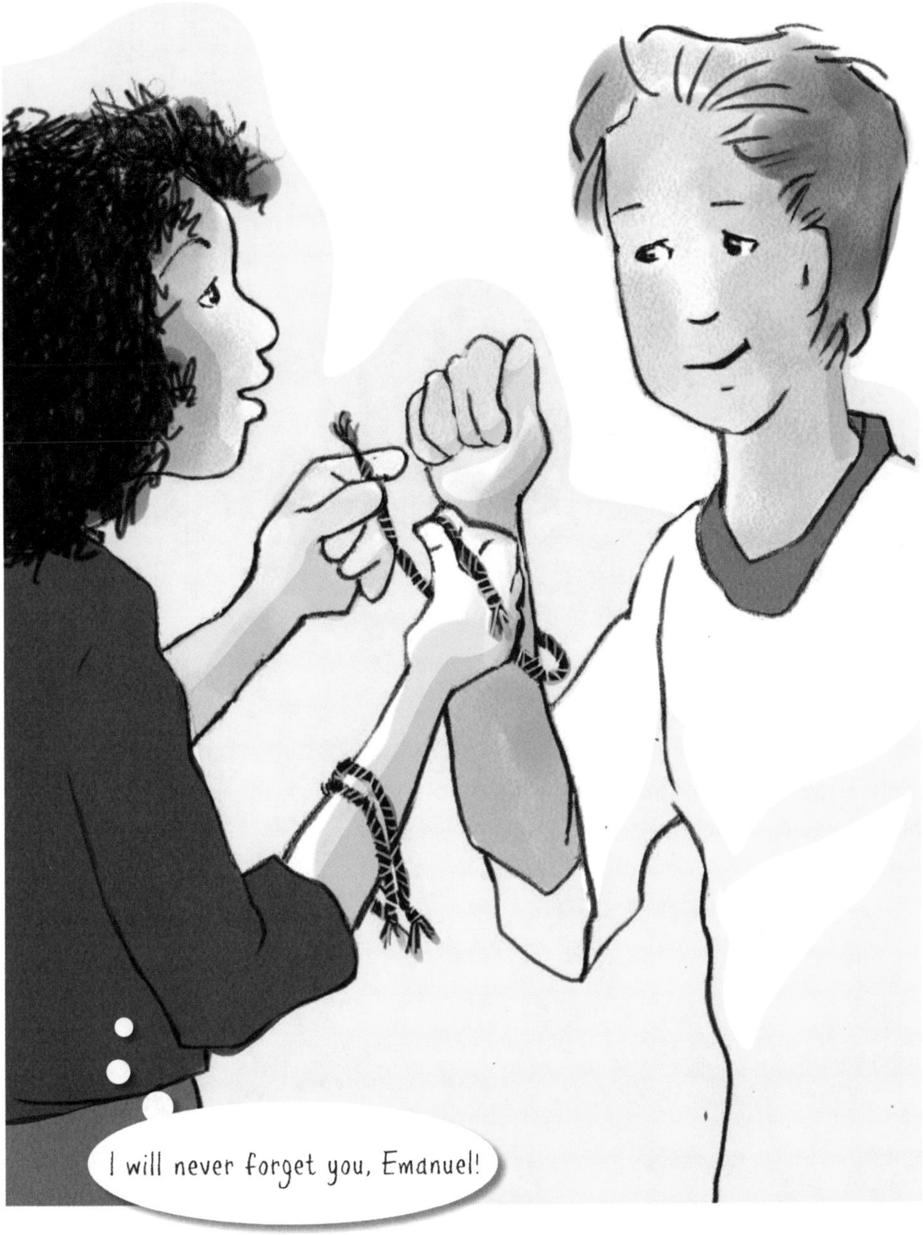
I will never forget you, Emanuel!

It was a sunny day when the truck brought furniture to our new home.

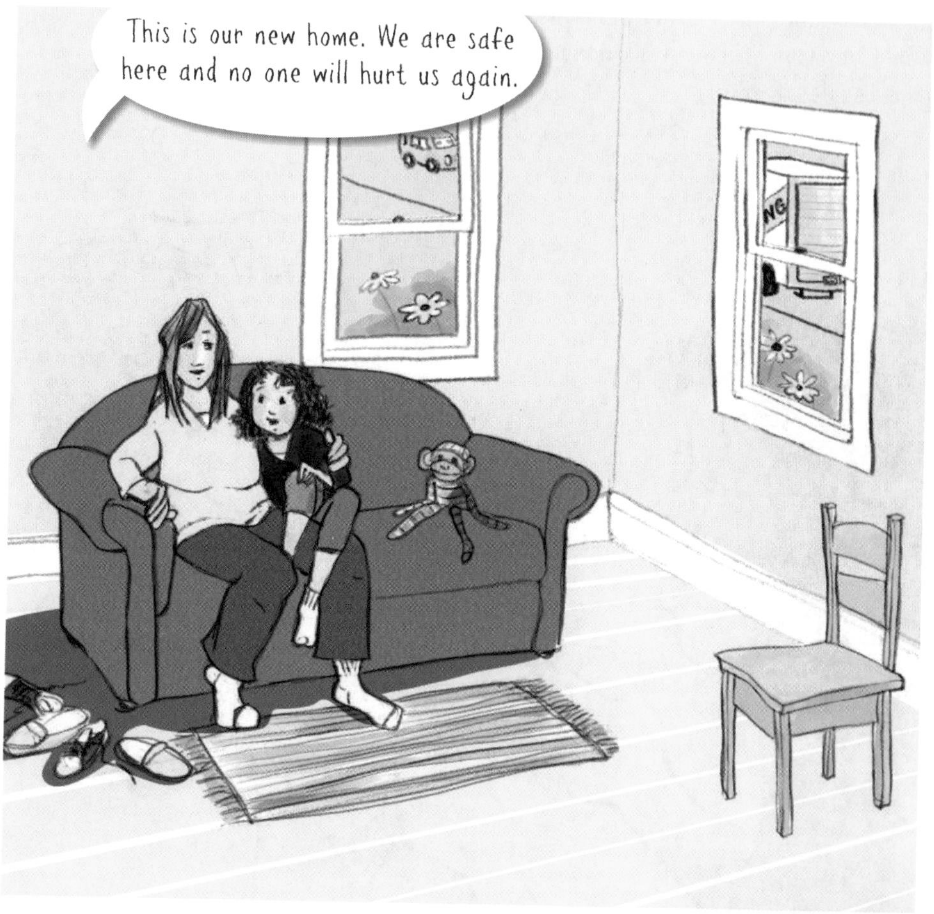
This is our new home. We are safe here and no one will hurt us again.

That night Mom and I slept in the same bed. She hugged me as I cried.

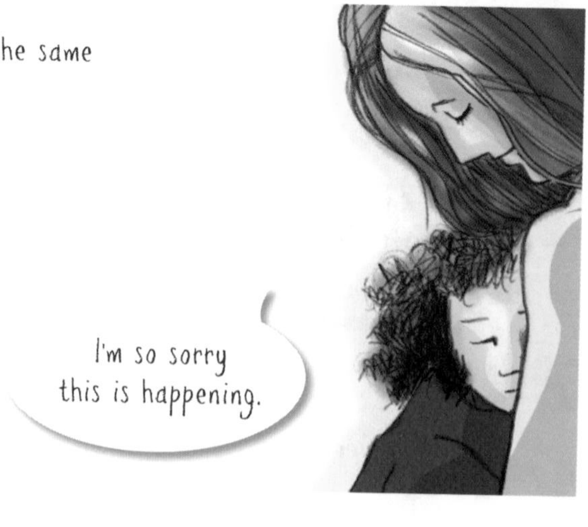
I'm so sorry this is happening.

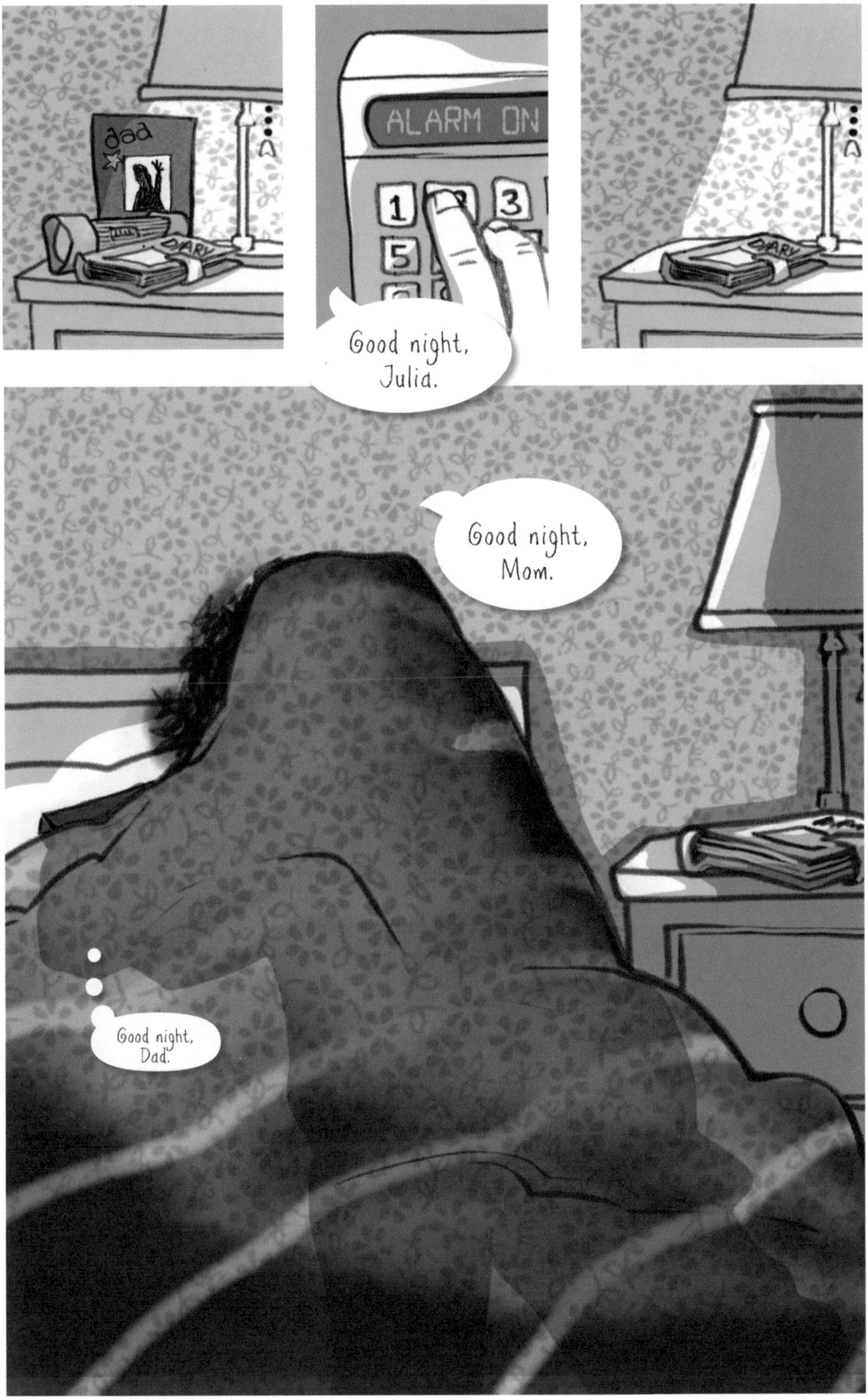
dad
DIARY
ALARM ON
1
3
5
Good night, Julia.
Good night, Mom.
Good night, Dad.

The next morning while we had breakfast Mom said a counsellor named Lori would be coming to the house. A counsellor? Was I crazy? Mom explained that to stay in safe housing we both had to talk to counsellors. Another rule was that we could not have men older than 18 in our house.

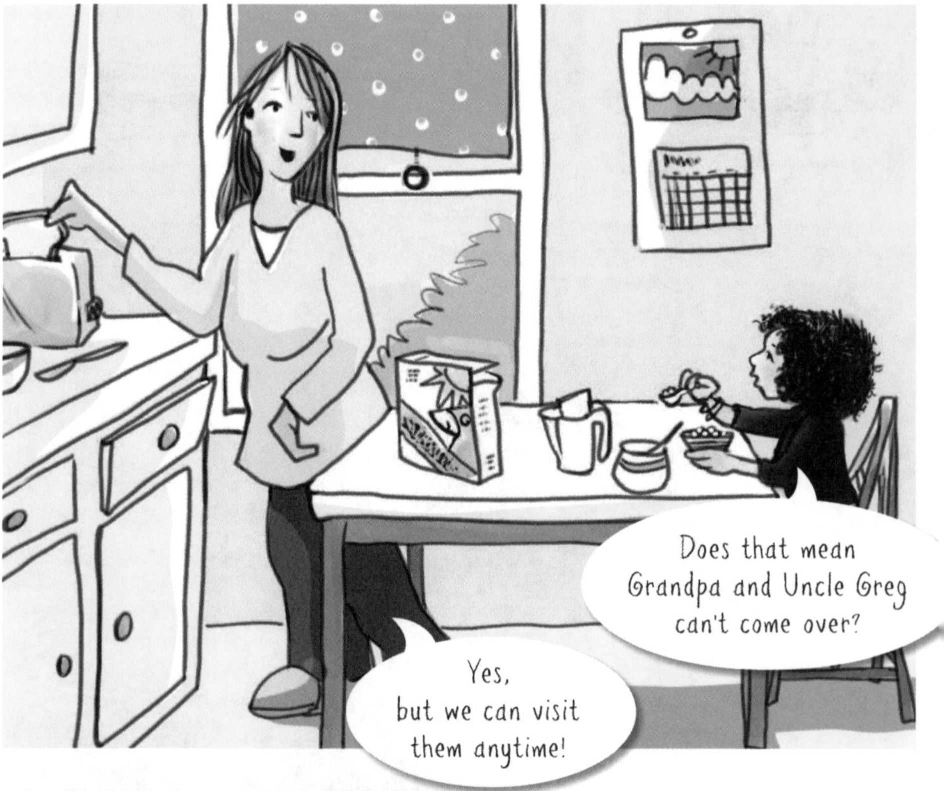
Does that mean Grandpa and Uncle Greg can't come over?
Yes, but we can visit them anytime!

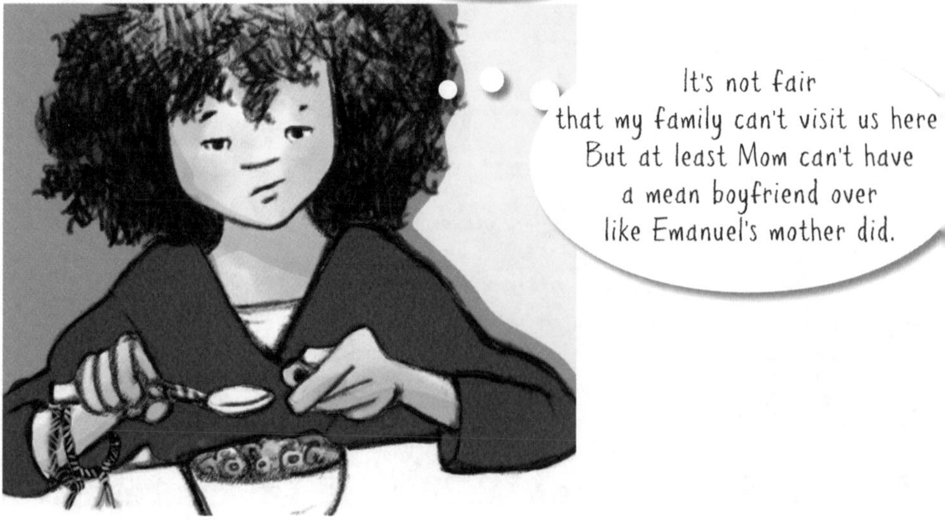
It's not fair that my family can't visit us here But at least Mom can't have a mean boyfriend over like Emanuel's mother did.

When Lori was at our house she was so cool I didn't think she was a counsellor. She told me I was allowed to tell her anything and I wouldn't get into trouble for it. I looked at Mom. She actually agreed!

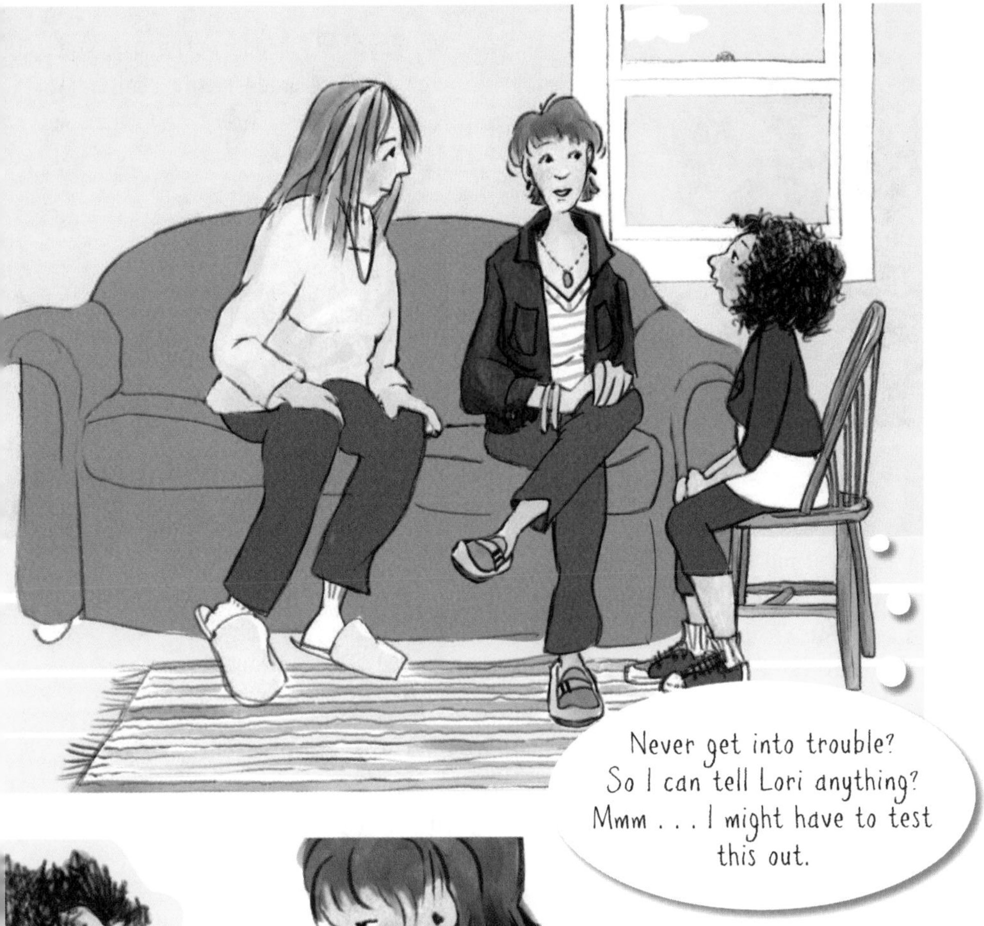
Never get into trouble? So I can tell Lori anything? Mmm . . . I might have to test this out.

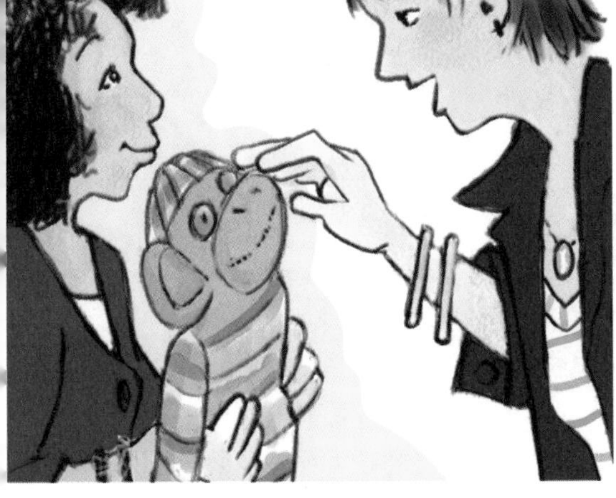

I had to change schools, and Mom told my new teacher and principal we live in safe housing. They had to know because Dad is not allowed to pick me up without Mom's permission.

My first time at Lori's office was weird! I was really nervous. She showed me around and introduced me to everyone. I was to see her once a week so we could talk about my feelings and I could have group activities with the other kids.

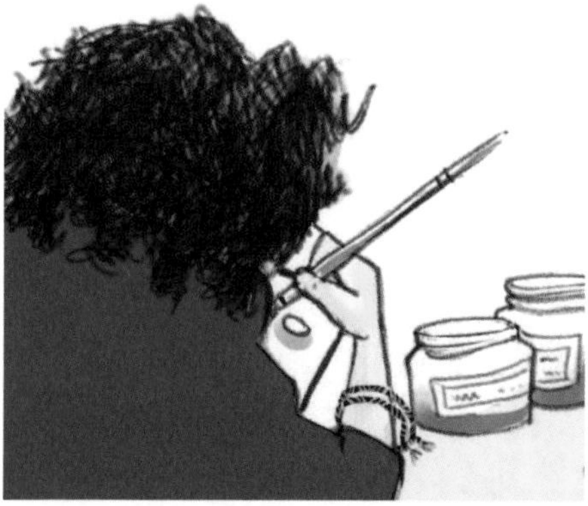

My favourite group activity is Art. One time we made really cool masks. My mask showed how I felt when my dad hurt my mom.

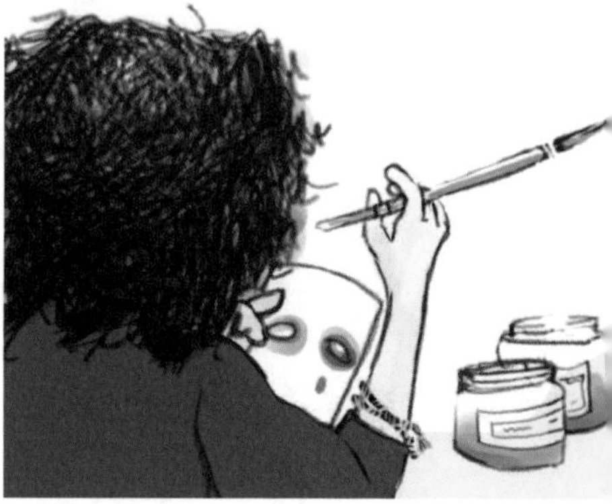

Another group activity is just talking. The first time was about abuse. One kid said, "My dad is all grown up. He should know better." We learned that if someone hurts us, we should tell an adult we trust, like a teacher or the police.

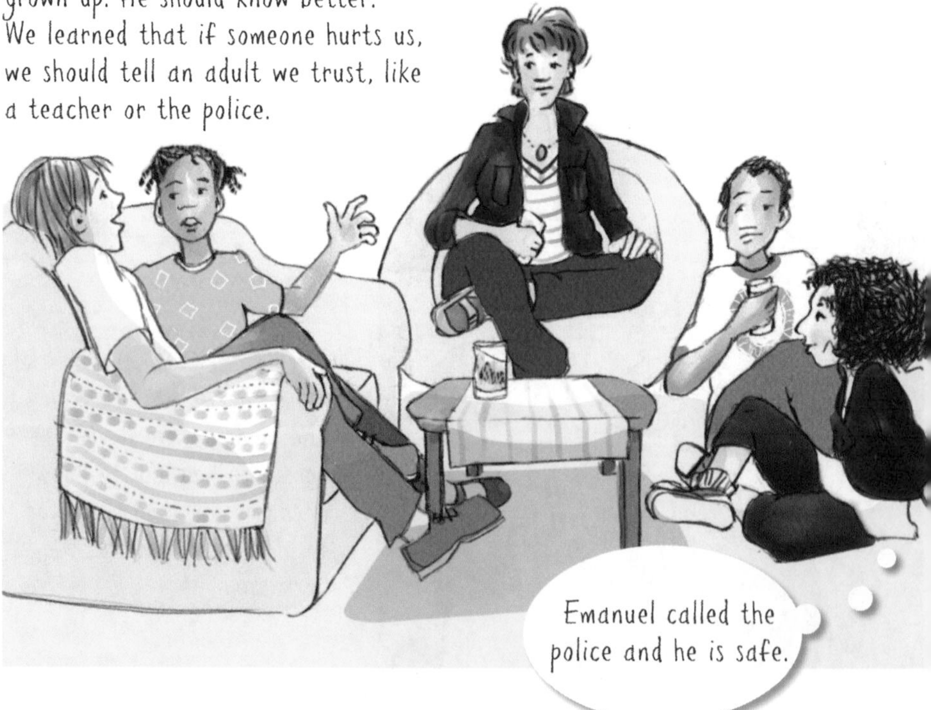
Emanuel called the police and he is safe.

Sometimes, all of the families get together to play games.

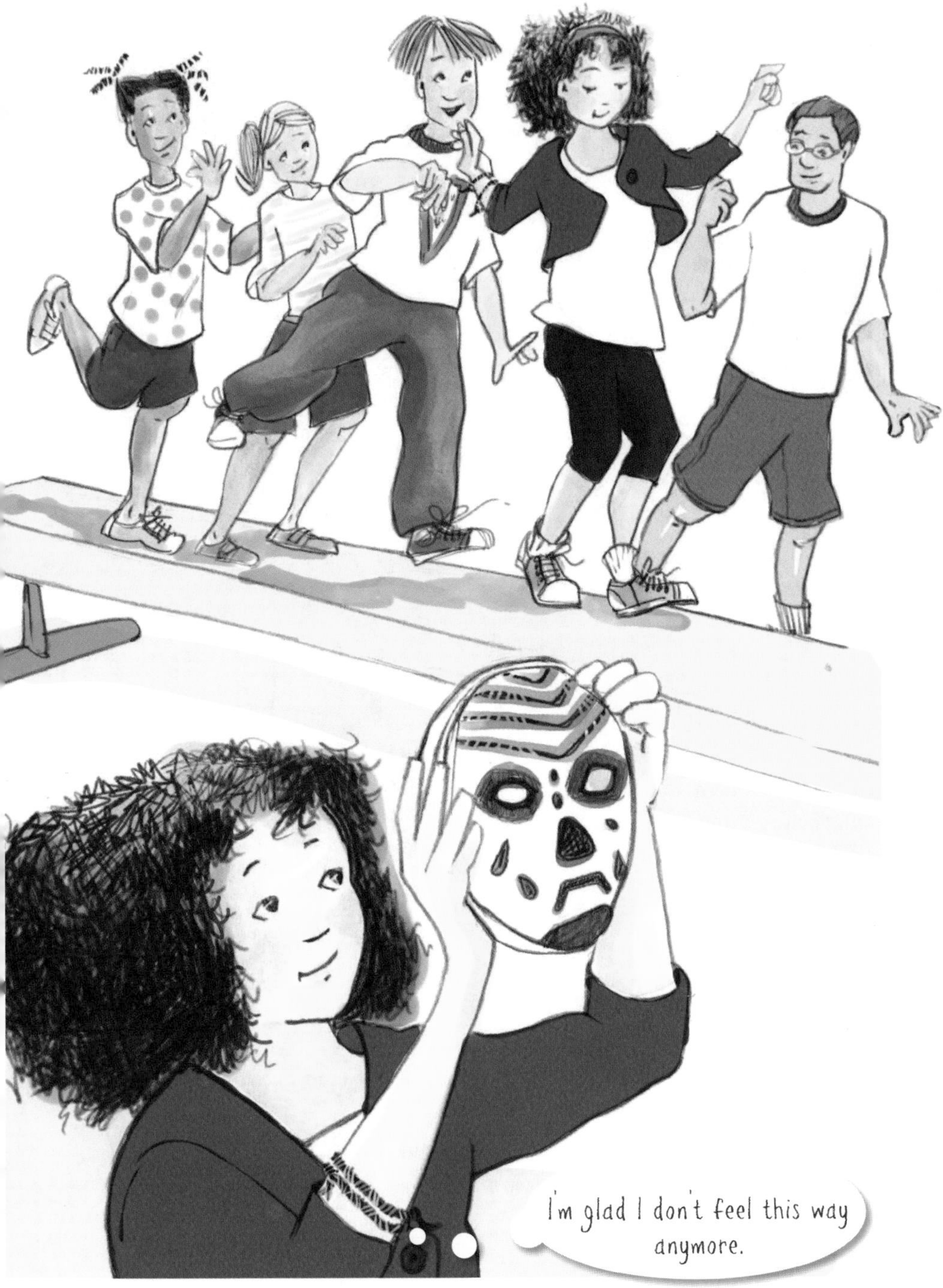
I'm glad I don't feel this way anymore.

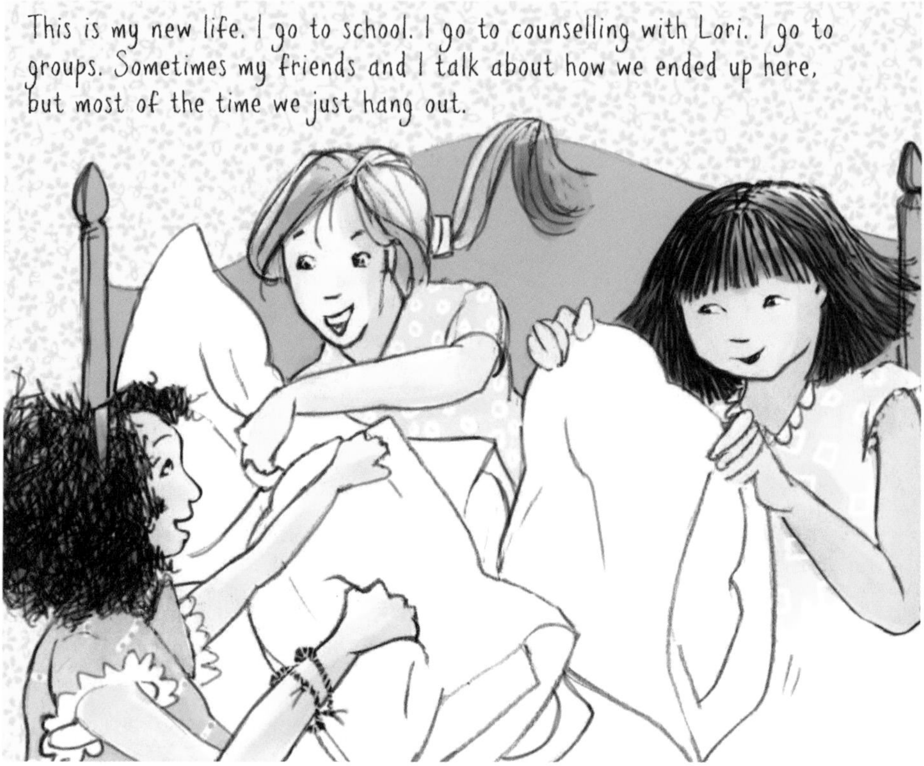
This is my new life. I go to school. I go to counselling with Lori. I go to groups. Sometimes my friends and I talk about how we ended up here, but most of the time we just hang out.

After a while I started to see my dad on the weekends. At first I didn't want to go because I felt guilty.

Dad doesn't know where we live or our phone number. He and Mom speak through email. Mom says this is best for now.

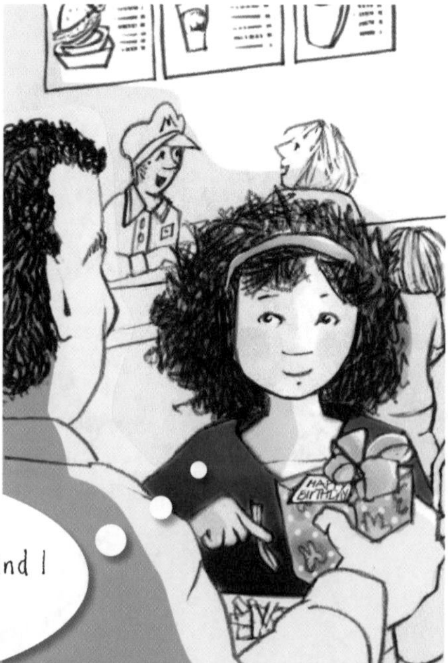
This is weird. But at least I get to see Dad and I don't get stomach aches any more.

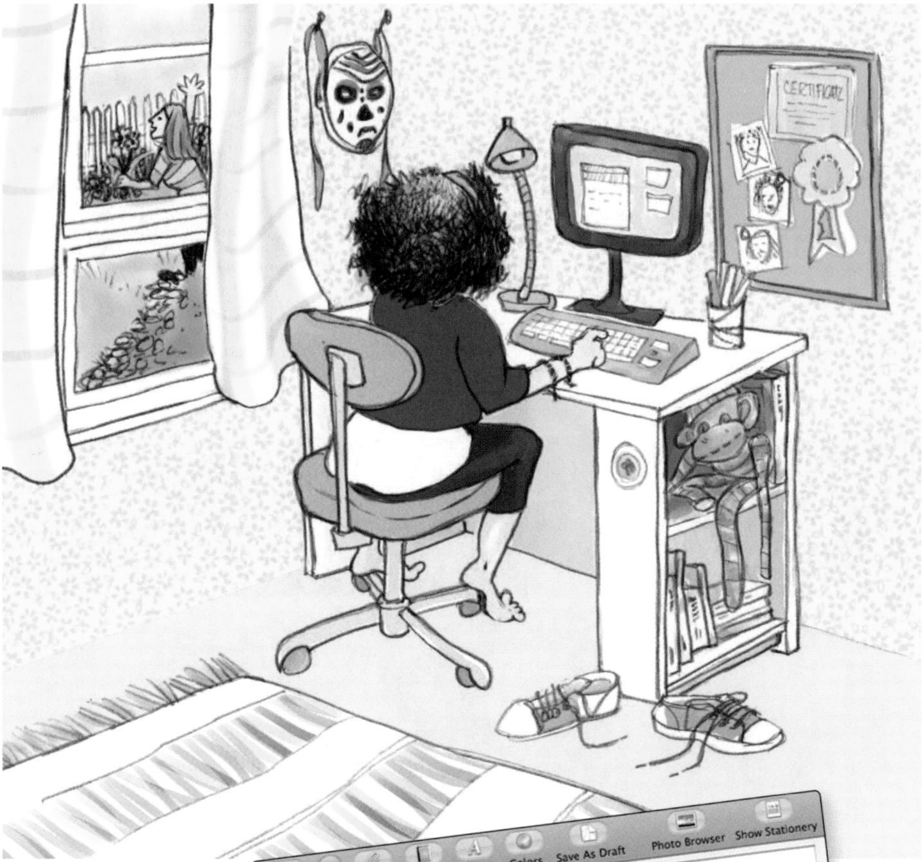

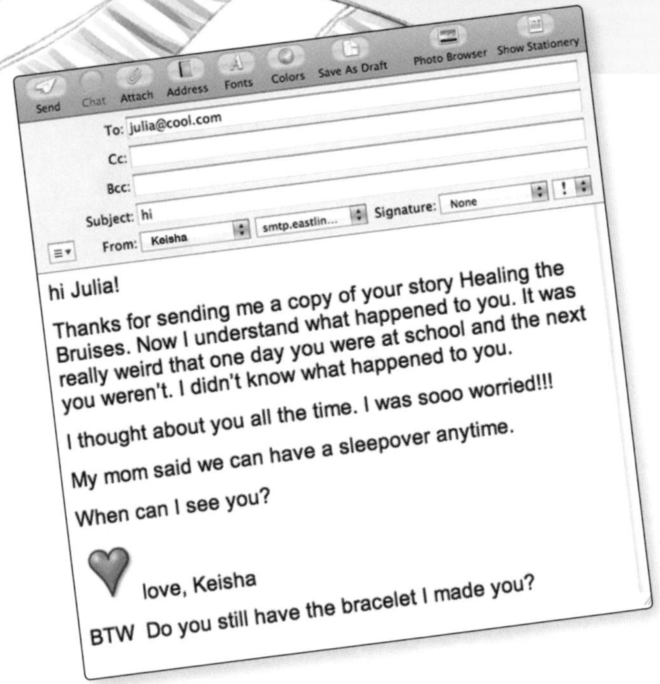
Send
Chat
Attach
Address
Fonts
Colors
Save As Draft
Photo Browser
Show Stationery

To: julia@cool.com
Cc:
Bcc:
Subject: hi
From: Keisha
smtp.eastlin...
Signature: None

hi Julia!

Thanks for sending me a copy of your story Healing the Bruises. Now I understand what happened to you. It was really weird that one day you were at school and the next you weren't. I didn't know what happened to you.

I thought about you all the time. I was sooo worried!!!

My mom said we can have a sleepover anytime.

When can I see you?

love, Keisha

BTW Do you still have the bracelet I made you?

Second stage housing exists in most major centres across Canada. This story is based on the experiences of a woman and child who were helped by Alice Housing. Founded in Halifax, NS in 1983, Alice Housing provides safe second stage housing and supportive counselling for women and children leaving domestic violence. Created in 2006 by Joanne Bernard and creatively named by Tina Riley, Alice Housing's Healing the Bruises program encourages child witnesses/victims of domestic violence to process and overcome their experiences while showing them that violence does not have to frame their future or define their legacy.

For a list of second stage housing options, links to helpful resources and classroom discussion resources, please go to:
www.formac.ca/HealingtheBruises

Acknowledgements

This is a work of fiction that has been created with knowledge obtained through our work with children from abusive homes.

Any resemblance to actual events or persons is coincidental but possible, as the occurrences of similar events in these situations is common.

8/14 ~~Central Children's Department~~
coping

1 9114